Wolf Comes to Town

For Gemma, Jade, Kate and Lucy

A Red Fox Book
Published by Random House Children's Books
20 Vauxhall Bridge Road, London SW1V 2SA
A division of The Random House Group Ltd
London Melbourne Sydney Auckland
Johannesburg and agencies throughout the world

3 5 7 9 10 8 6 4 2

First published in Great Britain by Hutchinson Children's Books 1994
Red Fox edition 2000

Printed in Singapore by Tien Wah Press (PTE) Ltd

THE RANDOM HOUSE GROUP Ltd Reg. No. 954009
www.randomhouse.co.uk

Wolf Comes to Town

Denis Manton

There was once a wolf who came to live in the hills close to a town. It was only a short bus ride to the shops, but whenever the wolf left his house to go shopping he dressed in disguise, for he knew that people didn't like wolves.

The wolf could dress up in a hundred different ways. He had a rackful of clothes: suits, dresses and shirts of every kind; he had wigs, gloves, a cupboard full of shoes, and an amazing variety of hats.

He could appear to be a sweet old lady, a fat bearded man, or a smart young woman, and when he caught the bus nobody suspected who he *really* was.

Once he got to the town, the wolf didn't bother about paying for anything. He'd just go into the shops and browse around until he saw something that he liked.

Then he would say, 'I like it, I *want* it, and I'LL TAKE IT!'

And he'd show his great teeth, snatch up the goods, and dash back to his home.

The wolf stole all kinds of things: carpets, lamb chops, books, toys, a stereo and lots of ice cream.

He stole a guitar, saucepans and everything else that he wanted, and would lie in bed sipping stolen drinks, eating stolen chocolates and laughing at his favourite TV shows on his stolen TV.

Shopkeepers became wary of their customers. A smart young woman was often bundled out of shops just because she had a suspiciously long nose . . .

. . . and there was a fat man with a beard who was shut out of every restaurant in the town.

One day a policeman came into a posh picture gallery and warned the owner that the wolf was somewhere in the town. 'Take care to keep your doors locked tight,' he said. 'He's a clever devil that wolf, and you can't afford to lose any of these paintings.'

'Great heavens!' the owner said, and he ordered some students to leave his gallery at once. 'Get out! All of you! Go on! Clear off!'

He turned and thanked the policeman for the warning. 'I'm not taking any chances,' he said. 'These paintings are valuable – especially that one there,' and he pointed to a picture of a sailing ship.

'Yes, that's a very fine picture,' the policeman said, and he bent forward to get a closer look.

'I like it, I *want* it, and I'LL TAKE IT!' he snarled, and the wolf seized the painting with his paws and ran from the gallery, leaving the owner quaking with terror.

Pet cats began to disappear. Sometimes the cats had only strayed for a while and then came home again, but some cats *never* came home.

Then small dogs began to vanish. People wondered whether the wolf was responsible and were horrified to think that their pets might have … *might have been eaten!*

One morning, three women sat on a bench by the pond. They fed pieces of bread to the ducks, and they pined for their lost pets.

One of them said that she had lost all three of her cats. 'I miss them so much,' she wept. 'Tiny, Ginger and Sheba. Such *nice* cats they were.' The other women wept too.

'Such nice *plump* cats,' said a sweet old lady, dabbing her eye with a hanky. 'Especially Sheba. *But she wasn't as plump as these ducks!*'

The other two women rummaged in their bags to find more pieces of bread. When they looked up, the sweet old lady had gone, and so had the ducks, leaving just a few feathers floating on the pond.

On his way home, the wolf laughed and licked his lips.
'I liked them, I *caught* 'em and I *ATE* 'EM!' he sang.

That evening there was a garden party. The children enjoyed themselves, but shopkeepers were angry, pet-owners were troubled and even parents became worried. 'Whatever next?!' they asked. 'If we don't do something about that wolf, he might start eating our *children!*'

'Burn him!' a little boy shouted. 'Burn the wolf and then drown him! Cut his ears off! Pull his teeth out and chop his head off!'

His mother smiled fondly and said, 'What a brave boy.'

Everyone agreed that the little boy was *very* brave.

The parson patted the boy's head and said, 'That's the spirit, son. I like you. What's your name?'

'My name's Bernard,' the boy shouted, 'and I'm not scared of a silly, stupid old wolf!'

When the light faded it was time to go home, but little Bernard was missing. He wasn't at the party and couldn't be found anywhere, so people brought torches and began searching the hills around the town.

They searched all night, and it was almost morning before they discovered the wolf's house.

Peering inside a room, they saw an untidy jumble.

'There's my stolen carpet!' a shopkeeper whispered.

'My grandfather clock!' another shopkeeper said.

Shopkeepers rushed into the house and claimed their stolen goods. 'My saucepans!' 'My stereo!' 'My guitar!' 'My TV!' they shouted.

'Little Bernard's little trousers!' his mother wailed, but she was pushed aside by the gallery owner who grabbed his valuable painting.

In the wolf's bedroom they found a shopping trolley full of stolen toys, and they saw the wolf's disguises. There were suits, dresses, shirts, wigs, gloves, ties, shoes, and hats of all sorts.

'We'd better throw these clothes away,' a policewoman said.

'No, the wolf might find them,' a postman said. 'Let's bury them.'

'No, the wolf might dig them up,' a fireman said. 'Let's burn them.'

'No, that would be a waste,' a nurse said. 'There are plenty of poor people who would be glad to wear these things. Help me load them into this shopping trolley, and I'll put them in a jumble sale.'

The trolley was soon packed and the nurse pushed it out of the house. 'They're lovely clothes,' she said ....

'I like them, I *want* them, and . . .

. . . I'LL TAKE THEM TO ANOTHER TOWN!'